With my thanks to Margaret Cotton
of the City of Birmingham Symphony Orchestra
for musical advice for mice,
and to Hugo Nightingale who kindly lent me
his model narrowboat.

First published in Great Britain 1986
by Methuen Children's Books Ltd
11 New Fetter Lane, London EC4P 4EE
Copyright © 1986 Heather S. Buchanan
Printed in Great Britain

ISBN 0 416 53920 3

George Mouse's Water Music

Heather S. Buchanan

Methuen Children's Books

One fine Spring afternoon George Mouse was wandering home along the riverbank looking for primroses, when he came across an enormous brown kettle. It caught his eye because it was painted all over with orange and yellow flowers and looked very cheerful. He sat down beside it to look at it more carefully. Then he snapped off a reed which was growing at the water's edge, and nibbled along it thoughtfully.

Through the long grass he could see a narrowboat, moored a little further downstream, and he guessed that the kettle belonged to the people on the boat. He blew softly down the reed, moving his paws up and down past the holes he had nibbled. A lovely musical sound came out, and suddenly George had an idea.

"I could make a narrowboat," he thought, "and I could play music as I travelled along the river. For everyone to hear."

So George began to make plans, and scampered home to make them happen.

George had a workshop under the roots of the tree stump where he and his family lived. It was full of useful bits and pieces. He loved making things. Before long he was whistling away, drawing a plan, choosing wood and hammering it together. A boat with a roof and windows began to take shape, and he leaned it against flower stems to hold it until it was all bolted together. His five sisters came to see, asking lots of questions and trying to jump on board. George was happy because his plan was working well, so he didn't mind them watching.

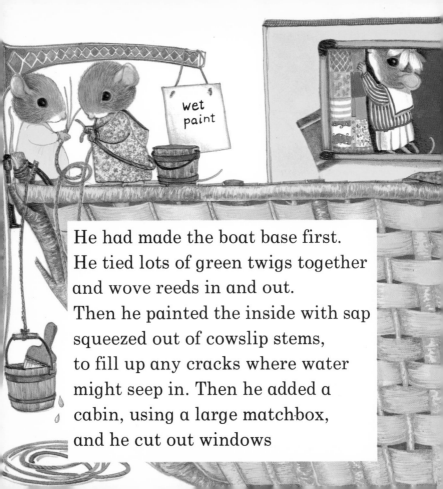

He had made the boat base first.
He tied lots of green twigs together
and wove reeds in and out.
Then he painted the inside with sap
squeezed out of cowslip stems,
to fill up any cracks where water
might seep in. Then he added a
cabin, using a large matchbox,
and he cut out windows

wet
paint

on each side with his saw. He
added a rudder for steering, and
painted patterns on it with
a mixture of squeezed berries
and catkin pollen. Cowslip
and Daisy wove ropes from
plaited grass, whilst Bryony,
Campanula and Clover
sewed patchwork curtains.

George was so pleased with his boat that he kept jumping up and down. He had secretly made musical instruments for each of his sisters. For Bryony he had made a mandolin from a beechnut and a matchstick, for Clover, shakers made from dried poppy heads and seeds, for Cowslip another reed flute, for Campanula

a triangle made from two hairpins, and lastly for little Daisy, a wonderful wooden drum. George had made himself an impressive baton to conduct with, using a fishbone he had found and polished.

At last they were off! They rolled the boat to the water's edge and launched it with a big splash. George told everyone to hold on tight as they perched in a row on the roof. George's father walked along the bank, pulling them with Daisy's rope whilst they tried out their instruments. Some made musical noises, some made strange noises, and Campanula got her nose caught in the triangle, so she didn't make a noise at all.

They managed to play something which sounded like *A Frog He Would A-wooing Go* after a lot of puffing and banging and quite a lot of argument. Their mother came out often with acorn juice for them and said how nice it all sounded. Daisy went on beating her drum all the time, even when the others had stopped playing. George was just beginning to look rather cross.

Their mother said she thought they were so good that they could give a performance. But first she wanted them to have something to eat to keep their strength up. She called to Father Mouse who tied the boat securely to a flower stem which was overhanging the water, and she brought out a seedcake, and berry jam, and more acorn juice. George and his sisters were so excited they could hardly eat!

It was time to start. Suddenly George felt terribly shy, but when he saw the others scampering aboard and tuning up their instruments, he stood proudly by the tiller and took up his fishbone.
He tapped twice on the deck, Father Mouse tugged on the rope, and they began. It was not long before lots of animals came running out to see them.

Everything was going splendidly.
Animals were cheering all along the bank.
But George was so busy conducting and
feeling important that he did not see a
branch hanging low over the river. As the
boat passed under it, his stripey suit was
caught and in a flash he was whisked up
into the air. For a long moment he hung
suspended upside down, and then fell
headfirst with a splash into the cold, cold
water.

George was terrified as the current carried him swiftly upstream, but luckily his sisters came to the rescue. "Mouse overboard!" they shouted, and at once their father stopped the boat. Then Daisy threw her wooden drum down to George, and Clover shouted "hold on, hold on" as he went under again. She jumped in and caught hold of his tail, paddling with him to the drum. Then she pulled him across to the bank using her feet as propellers.

All was well in the end. The mice fished George and Clover out and wrapped them in warm towels, and their mother brewed up some acorn tea to warm them. George's sisters told him how brave he was and took up their instruments again to play "For he's a Jolly Good Fellow", ending with three cheers for George.

As they floated home, George felt very happy, and already he was busy with new plans – an expedition to find where the river joined the sea, and an idea for making life-jackets out of hollowed-out conkers.

When they reached the bank at Tree
Stump House George was fast asleep.
They carried him home gently and put his
bed in front of the fire, to keep him warm
all night whilst he dreamt of his next
adventure.